Alone in a

"It's silly to be afraid," Jessica said bravely. "We're all alone in here. What could hurt us?"

"Nothing, I guess," Elizabeth agreed. "We're the only ones in the whole store."

Jessica's eyes lit up. "Did you hear what you just said?" she asked. "We have the entire store to ourselves! We can do whatever we want!"

"Except get out," Elizabeth said.

"Someone will find us soon," Jessica said. "Until then, we might as well have fun."

"What should we do?" Elizabeth asked.

"Play!" Jessica said.

Bantam Books in the SWEET VALLEY KIDS series

SWEET VALLEY KIDS
SUPER SPECIAL

TRAPPED IN TOYLAND

Written by
Molly Mia Stewart

Created by
FRANCINE PASCAL

Illustrated by
Ying-Hwa Hu

BANTAM BOOKS
NEW YORK · TORONTO · LONDON · SYDNEY · AUCKLAND

To Benjamin Simon Doherty

RL 2, 005-008

TRAPPED IN TOYLAND
A Bantam Book / December 1994

Sweet Valley High® and Sweet Valley Kids are
trademarks of Francine Pascal

Conceived by Francine Pascal

Produced by Daniel Weiss Associates, Inc.
33 West 17th Street
New York, NY 10011

Cover art by Susan Tang

ISBN: 0-553-48251-3

Published simultaneously in the United States and Canada

Bantam Books are published by Bantam Books, a division of Bantam
Doubleday Dell Publishing Group, Inc. Its trademark, consisting of the
words "Bantam Books" and the portrayal of a rooster, is Registered in U.S.
Patent and Trademark Office and in other countries. Marca Registrada.
Bantam Books, 1540 Broadway, New York, New York 10036.

PRINTED IN THE UNITED STATES OF AMERICA

CWO   0 9 8 7 6 5 4 3 2 1

CHAPTER 1

Christmas Magic

Elizabeth Wakefield took a deep breath. "Yummy!" she exclaimed. "It smells like Christmas."

"It *smells* like Christmas?" Elizabeth's twin sister, Jessica, asked. "What are you talking about? We're in a car. It smells like a car."

"Even if we were outside, it would smell like palm trees," Steven, the twins' older brother, added. "It's eighty-five degrees out. Christmas is supposed to smell like pine trees and snow."

Living in Sweet Valley, California, meant it was warm all year, even at Christmastime.

"You guys have no imagination," Elizabeth said with a sigh.

Jessica laughed. "Well, I think it *feels* like Christmas. I'm so excited, I can hardly sit still."

"Me, too," Elizabeth agreed.

Elizabeth and Jessica often agreed. That might have been because not only were they twins, they were *identical* twins. Both girls had blue-green eyes and long blond hair with bangs. It was hard to tell them apart. Sometimes the twins even fooled their family into thinking that Jessica was Elizabeth, and Elizabeth was Jessica.

But the twins disagreed at least as much as they agreed. That's because their personalities were very different. Elizabeth enjoyed reading and playing soccer. Jessica liked dolls and pretending to be a ballerina. Elizabeth waited patiently to open her presents on Christmas morning. Jessica spent the week before Christmas shaking her packages and trying to guess what was inside. Even when they picked matching outfits, Elizabeth chose hers in green, and Jessica insisted on pink.

But those differences didn't matter to Elizabeth and Jessica. The twins shared a bedroom, they shared clothes and toys, and they shared secrets that nobody else knew. They were best friends.

"Are we there yet?" Elizabeth called to her parents, who were sitting in the front seats.

"Almost," Mr. Wakefield replied. He flicked on the right-turn signal in the family's van and started to change lanes. "This is our exit off the highway."

"Yippee!" Jessica cried.

It was Christmas Eve. The Wakefields were on their way to Evelyn's, a new department store near Los Angeles. The store had just opened, but a few of the twins' friends had already visited it.

"Ellen Riteman told me that Evelyn's toy department is amazing,"

Jessica reported. "It takes up almost the entire first floor of the store!"

"Eva Simpson said that she had never seen so many toys all in one place," Elizabeth added.

"I can't wait to get there," Jessica said.

"I'm excited, too," Elizabeth said.

"Let's go to the toy department first," Steven suggested.

"Definitely!" Jessica agreed.

"And then we'll shop for our secret," Elizabeth added in a low voice. She didn't want anyone but Jessica to hear what she was saying.

Jessica and Elizabeth had a big secret. They were planning to buy Mrs. Wakefield's Christmas present at Evelyn's.

The twins had already taken care of their other presents. Elizabeth had written a story for Steven, and Jessica drew pictures for it. The girls had made a picture frame out of construction paper for their father. A few days earlier, the twins had wrapped the picture frame and

4

homemade book in pretty paper. Then they had placed the gifts under the Wakefields' Christmas tree.

But Elizabeth and Jessica had not thought of anything they could make for Mrs. Wakefield. They hadn't found anything special enough to buy her in Sweet Valley, either. Jessica and Elizabeth were certain they would have better luck at Evelyn's. The twins' friends had made the new store sound magical.

"Do you still have the money?" Elizabeth whispered to Jessica.

"Yes," Jessica replied. She shook her pink satin change purse so that the money inside clinked together. The twins had been saving their allowances for weeks and weeks. They had saved an entire $15.63.

All of the money was in Jessica's change purse. The twins had agreed that Jessica would carry the money until they found the perfect present for their mother. Then it would be time to spend it!

"We're here," Mrs. Wakefield announced.

Mr. Wakefield drove past a huge red sign that read EVELYN'S. He drove around and around the big parking lot until he found an empty spot.

Jessica, Elizabeth, Steven, and their parents got out of the car and started the long walk toward the store.

"Wow," Elizabeth said when they got close.

A choir was standing outside Evelyn's main entrance. The dozens of singers were dressed like elves. They were singing "Jingle Bell Rock" in three-part harmony.

As the Wakefields approached, one of the elves handed small candy canes to Elizabeth, Jessica, and Steven.

"Thanks!" Jessica said with a big smile. Elizabeth knew her sister loved candy canes.

The Wakefields listened to the choir sing several songs. Then they headed toward Evelyn's main entrance. As they passed through the door, a shower of plastic snow fell on them.

"It's snowing!" Elizabeth said, giggling.

"This is cool," Jessica added.

The inside of the store was covered with snow and icicles. An enormous Christmas tree covered with white lights and red bows stood opposite the entrance. There were even snowmen!

Mrs. Wakefield smiled. "It's a winter wonderland."

"Pretty neat for California," Mr. Wakefield said.

Elizabeth took a deep breath. "That Christmas tree smells fantastic."

"Now I don't need imagination to get into the holiday spirit," Jessica said. "This store really does smell like Christmas!"

Steven ran a few steps ahead. "I see the toy department," he called to the twins. "Hurry up!"

Jessica grabbed Mr. Wakefield's hand.

Elizabeth grabbed Mrs. Wakefield's hand.

"Come on!" the twins said together. They pulled their parents toward the toy department. Mr. and Mrs. Wakefield allowed themselves to be dragged along.

Two giant nutcracker dolls were guarding the entrance to the toy department. People were streaming in and out. The Wakefields joined the river of people. Seconds later, they were inside the toy department.

"Wow," Steven said. "Video games!"

"Look at that stuffed zebra," Elizabeth said. "It's bigger than a real one!"

"Check out the cars!" Jessica yelled. "They're almost big enough to be real, too!" She ran toward three shiny convertibles.

Steven ran after Jessica.

"Stay in the toy department, kids," Mr. Wakefield called. "We'll find you when we're ready to go," Mrs. Wakefield added.

"OK, Mom and Dad," Elizabeth said. Then she sprinted after Steven and Jessica.

Jessica ran up to the cars. Steven and Elizabeth were right behind her.

"Wow!" Jessica said. "They're actually big enough to get into."

"It looks like they really work," Elizabeth added. "There's a steering wheel and pedals and everything."

"I want to get in one," Steven said.

"You can't," Elizabeth pointed out. "There are ribbons tied across the seats so that you can't sit down."

"I guess the store doesn't want us to climb inside," Jessica said. "I wonder why."

Steven picked up the price tag on one of the cars. He let out a low whistle. "Maybe it's because these are really *expensive*," he said. "They cost—"

"WHAT DO YOU THINK YOU'RE DOING?"

Steven and the twins spun around. A tall balding man was hurrying toward them. He looked furious.

9

CHAPTER 2

The World's Best Toy Department

"Put that down!" the man yelled.

Steven dropped the price tag. "Who are you?" he asked.

"I'm the store manager," the man said. "What are you doing here?"

The manager was wearing a blue suit. He had a walkie-talkie attached to his belt. He was also wearing a pin with his name printed on it. *Mr. Fegato,* Jessica read.

"I asked what you're doing here!" the manager yelled.

"It's Christmas Eve," Steven said with a shrug. "We're shopping."

"Do you have any money?" the store manager asked.

"No," Steven admitted.

"If you don't have the money to buy, *don't touch*," the manager bellowed.

"Geez," Elizabeth whispered to Jessica. "What happened to his Christmas spirit?"

"I heard that!" the manager yelled. "Don't talk to me about Christmas! Just stay away from these cars!"

Just then, the manager's walkie-talkie let out a piercing noise. "We have a suspected robbery," came a scratchy voice.

"A robbery?" Elizabeth asked. Her eyes were wide.

Mr. Fegato groaned. "Don't worry," he said. "I'm sure it's just another false alarm. Christmas really makes people act nuts." With that, he rushed off.

"Talk about nuts," Steven said.

Jessica grabbed Elizabeth's arm. "Forget about him," she said. "I want to see the rest of the toy department."

"See you later, shrimps," Steven said. "I'm going to go look at the bicycles."

11

"Do you want to see the bikes?" Elizabeth asked Jessica.

"No way!" Jessica replied. "I want to see the dolls."

"OK," Elizabeth agreed. "But then *I* want to see the dump trucks."

"Fine," Jessica said. "But dolls first."

The twins didn't have much trouble finding the dolls. They took up two whole aisles of the toy department.

Jessica gazed at the endless display. She was overwhelmed. "I bet there are a million of them," she said.

"At least," Elizabeth said.

There were baby dolls with no clothes on and grown-up dolls in beautiful gowns. Some of the dolls winked, some cried, and some sang. One even burped! Elizabeth found a doll that was smaller than her fingernail. Jessica found one that was taller than Steven.

After a long time, the twins ran out of dolls to inspect. "I wonder what's in the next aisle," Jessica said.

But Elizabeth had already run ahead. Jessica caught up with her sister under a huge STOP sign.

"Check this out," Elizabeth said, sounding excited.

Elizabeth had found an aisle full of things that moved. There were space-ships and trains and boats and taxis and steam shovels and buses and skateboards and roller skates and ice skates.

The next aisle was full of board games.

The one after that was stuffed with stuffed animals—cats, dogs, birds, bears, horses, pigs, lions, tigers, giraffes, elephants, rhinos, dinosaurs, and raccoons.

"Look at this," Jessica said, picking up a stuffed animal between two fingers. "Who would want a stuffed snake?"

"Not me," Elizabeth admitted. "But I see lots of other things I like. I'm almost glad Mom and Dad said we couldn't buy anything. I'd never be able to choose."

"I would!" Jessica said.

14

Jessica and Elizabeth walked up an aisle full of Brenda stuff.

Brenda is that big pink rhino who has her own kids' show on TV. There were Brenda cassettes, Brenda videotapes, Brenda lunch boxes, Brenda stickers, and Brenda coloring books.

Elizabeth wrinkled her nose. "I don't like Brenda."

"I *hate* Brenda," Jessica said. "Especially when she sings."

"Beat you to the end of the aisle!" Elizabeth yelled.

The girls did their best to run down the aisle. It was hard because they had to dodge tons of tiny kids and their parents.

"I win!" Elizabeth yelled.

"I don't care," Jessica said. "I'm just happy to be out of Brenda-land."

The twins walked down the next aisle. It was full of basketballs and footballs and baseballs and soccer balls. At the end, Elizabeth and Jessica found

15

their parents talking to some other grown-ups.

"Are you having fun?" Mrs. Wakefield asked them.

"Yes!" Elizabeth said. "But we want to shop for something outside the toy department now."

"Shop for what?" Mr. Wakefield asked.

"It's a secret," Jessica told him. "We have to go alone."

"I see," Mr. Wakefield said.

Just then Steven ran up. "Mom! Dad!" he shouted. "I found something you've *got* to get me."

Mrs. Wakefield shook her head. "You know we just came here to look," she told Steven. "We aren't going to buy anything."

Elizabeth pulled on her father's hand. "Is it OK?" she asked. "Can Jessica and I go shopping by ourselves?"

"Not by yourselves," Mr. Wakefield replied. "But you may go with Steven."

"I don't want to go shopping with

them," Steven whined. "I want to play video games."

"Are you serious?" Elizabeth asked her brother. "The line for the video games is so long. There must be about a hundred kids in it."

Steven shrugged. "So?"

"Go with your sisters," Mrs. Wakefield told Steven. "You should be happy to do a favor for them. After all, it's almost Christmas."

"If I go with them, will you get me the game I want?" Steven asked.

"No," Mrs. Wakefield said firmly. "You'll go just to be nice."

Steven rolled his eyes. "Come on, shrimps," he said to the twins. "Let's make it fast."

"I want you kids to stay together," Mr. Wakefield said. "We'll meet in the house-wares department in an hour. It's on the seventh floor."

"What time is it now?" Jessica asked. "I don't have a watch."

"I don't have a watch, either," Elizabeth put in. "How will we know when an hour has gone by?"

"What would you babies do with watches?" Steven asked. "You hardly know how to tell time."

"That's not true!" Elizabeth protested.

"Well, it doesn't matter," Steven said importantly. "I'm wearing my watch. It's three thirty now. In an hour, it will be four thirty."

Mrs. Wakefield winked at the twins. "Very good, Steven."

"Have fun," Mr. Wakefield said. "See you later."

"Let's go," Steven said. He headed toward the entrance to the toy department. Jessica and Elizabeth ran to catch up with him.

CHAPTER 3

Last-Minute Squabbling

"Who do you shrimps want to get a present for?" Steven asked. "Me?"

"Not you," Elizabeth told him. "Mom."

"What are you going to get her?" Steven asked.

"We don't know yet," Jessica said.

"You don't know?" Steven sounded as if he were about to cry. "This is going to take forever."

"We just need to look around for a while," Elizabeth assured him.

"*Please* make it fast," Steven said. "I don't have all day. I've got to get back to the video games."

Jessica and Elizabeth exchanged looks. Shopping with Steven was not going to be easy.

"Let's take the elevator to the top floor," Jessica suggested. "Then we can work our way down."

"That sounds like fun," Elizabeth said.

Steven groaned. "It sounds like torture."

Still, Steven followed Jessica and Elizabeth to the elevators. When one came, they all got inside and rode to the eighth floor. That was the highest one.

"There's nothing up here but a snack bar," Jessica said.

"And a place to get your hair cut," Elizabeth added.

"Why don't you get Mom some shampoo for Christmas?" Steven suggested.

"No way," Elizabeth said.

"Fine," Steven said. "We're finished on this floor. Seven more to go." He started pushing the twins toward the escalator.

"I know what's on the seventh floor," Elizabeth said. "Housewares."

"Housewares are boring," Steven said. "Let's skip the seventh floor."

"No," Jessica said. "We might find something interesting."

Steven rolled his eyes.

On the seventh floor, Steven and the twins hurried through rows and rows of couches, tables, chairs, and beds. They also found a department that sold kitchen stuff.

"Salt and pepper shakers?" Steven suggested.

"We have salt and pepper shakers," Elizabeth pointed out.

"How about place mats?"

"Bor-ring," Jessica said.

"I told you," Steven said. "We should have skipped this floor. Let's go!"

"No, wait," Elizabeth said. "There's the book department. Maybe they have some books on furniture or something. Mom likes stuff like that."

The kids wandered through the book department. But they didn't find any books they thought Mrs. Wakefield would like.

"I wonder what's on the sixth floor," Jessica said as they took the escalator down.

Steven looked at a sign. "Stereos."

"We can't afford those," Jessica said.

"The fancy-food department is here, too," Steven announced. "Food is a good present."

"You just like to eat," Jessica told him.

"But Mom likes to cook," Elizabeth said. "Maybe that's not a bad idea."

On six, the twins examined hundreds of little spice packets. They looked at fancy spaghetti and fancy tea. There was lots of dried stuff: mushrooms, tomatoes, cranberries, and cherries.

"May I help you?" a salesman asked Jessica.

"Just tell me where the escalator is," Jessica replied. "This food is weird. I'm ready to hit the fifth floor."

Elizabeth read the store directory on the way down. The fifth floor had all different kinds of clothes on it.

"Keep going!" Steven yelled when they reached five. He jumped on the escalator down to the fourth floor. The twins didn't have time to stop him. Jessica and Elizabeth had no choice but to get on the escalator, too.

"You cheated," Elizabeth told Steven.

"I'm just trying to save you time," Steven said. "You don't want to buy Mom clothes."

"I guess you're right," Elizabeth admitted. "But don't do that again."

The fourth floor was crowded with sparkling makeup counters. Pretty women were standing near the escalator. They were spraying people with perfume as they walked by.

"Ooo, makeup!" Jessica exclaimed.

Steven and Elizabeth exchanged looks.

Elizabeth grabbed Jessica's hand. "We're not going to buy Mom makeup either," she reminded Jessica. "And we're running out of time."

"I just want to look for a second," Jessica pleaded.

Steven grabbed Jessica's other hand and pulled her back onto the escalator. "It's time to look at the third floor," he insisted.

"Fine," Jessica said. But she pouted all the way down to three.

The third floor had lots of interesting things on it. Jessica and Elizabeth looked at cozy robes and comfy slippers. They examined scarves and gloves and umbrellas.

"Get that red-and-blue scarf," Steven suggested.

"Do you really think Mom will like it?" Elizabeth asked.

Steven shrugged. "I just want you to buy something. Anything!"

"I want to see the second floor before we make a final decision," Jessica said.

"Great," Steven said. "That's perfect.

Why don't you look at everything in the whole store? Don't worry about me."

"Don't worry," Jessica said. "We won't."

Tucked away in the corner of one of the thousands of display cases on the second floor, Jessica and Elizabeth found Mrs. Wakefield's present. It was a wooden jewelry box with a blue satin lining.

"It's beautiful," Elizabeth said.

"I'm glad we didn't buy that stupid scarf," Jessica added.

"Hurry up and buy it," Steven demanded.

"Let's go find a salesperson," Elizabeth suggested.

Jessica glanced at the jewelry box. "If we all leave, someone else might buy it while we're gone."

"Then I'll stay here and guard it," Elizabeth said. "You go find a salesperson."

"Deal," Jessica said. She hurried off. A few minutes later, Jessica was back. She had an elderly saleswoman by the hand.

Jessica pointed to the jewelry box. "We want to buy that."

"It's going to be our mother's Christmas present," Elizabeth added with a happy grin.

"What a lovely choice," the saleswoman said. She reached into the display case and pulled out the jewelry box. "Shall I gift wrap it?"

"Um, just a second," Elizabeth said. "How much is it?"

The saleswoman squinted at the price tag. "With tax, it will come to about thirty-two dollars."

Jessica gasped.

"We don't have enough money," Elizabeth said. She was very disappointed.

"I'm sorry," the saleswoman said. "But I'm sure you'll find something else you like."

"Thanks," Jessica told her.

"Now what?" Steven asked.

"We have to pick out another present

for Mom," Elizabeth said. "After all, it *is* Christmas Eve."

"You've got about five minutes before we have to meet Mom and Dad," Steven said. "Hurry up and decide what to get."

"Let's go buy that scarf," Elizabeth suggested.

"A scarf is a boring present," Jessica said. "Let's get a pair of slippers with feathers on them. I saw some on the third floor."

"Don't be silly, Jessica," Elizabeth said. "Mom would never wear those. And we only have a few minutes to decide."

Jessica put her hands on her hips. "Mom would never wear that ugly scarf either!"

Steven groaned. "I'm going to get an ice-cream cone," he said. "There's supposed to be a stand somewhere on this floor. I'll be right back."

"You're not allowed to leave us by ourselves," Elizabeth reminded her brother.

"I'll be right back," Steven repeated.

"And if we get separated, we can just meet at the housewares department."

"But—" Jessica started.

"'Bye," Steven said. He wandered away.

The twins watched him go.

"We can decide what to buy while he's gone," Elizabeth told Jessica. "Which scarf did you like best?"

"I want to get slippers," Jessica insisted.

"Slippers are stupid," Elizabeth said.

The argument was just heating up again when a man wearing a pink baseball cap shoved Jessica aside, pushed through the crowd, and disappeared.

Jessica rubbed her arm. "That hurt," she complained. "Hey! Where's my purse?"

"You just had it," Elizabeth said.

"Well, it's gone now!" Jessica exclaimed. "And that means all of our money is gone!"

CHAPTER 4

A Long Winter's Nap

"We'll find your purse," Elizabeth promised Jessica. "But first we have to find Steven. Do you see him?"

Jessica stood on her tiptoes and looked around the busy store. "No," she said grumpily. "I can't believe he just left. He's such a pain sometimes."

"Steven said it was almost time for us to meet Mom and Dad," Elizabeth said. "I think we'd better go up to housewares."

Jessica stomped her foot. "We can't! We haven't gotten a present for Mom yet."

"But we don't have any money," Elizabeth pointed out.

"That's why we have to find my purse right now," Jessica insisted. "Then we'll buy Mom some slippers. *Then* we'll go up to housewares."

"Steven said we had to meet Mom and Dad in about five minutes," Elizabeth said. "I don't think we have time to do all that."

"We'll only be a few minutes late," Jessica said. "Come on. Start looking."

"OK," Elizabeth agreed. "But if we don't find the purse fast, we have to go meet Mom and Dad."

Jessica peeked under a display case. "Fine."

The twins searched the entire second floor. Then they took the escalator up to the third floor.

"We have to look for my purse everywhere we went with Steven," Jessica said.

"OK," Elizabeth agreed. "But hurry."

Slowly, the twins worked their way up to the sixth floor.

31

"Ouch!" Jessica yelled. She was crawling under a case on her hands and knees. A saleswoman had stepped on her fingers.

"What are you doing under there?" the saleswoman demanded.

"Looking for my purse," Jessica explained. "I lost it."

"Someone probably found it and turned it in," the saleswoman said. "You should look in Lost and Found. It's on the third floor near the bathrooms."

Elizabeth and Jessica hurried back down to the third floor. They found the bathrooms. Next to them was a door that said CUSTOMER SERVICE on it.

Jessica knocked.

"What do you want?" a nasty voice called.

The twins exchanged nervous looks.

"Come in and tell me what you want!" yelled the voice.

Jessica took a deep breath and pushed the door open. Elizabeth followed her.

The nasty voice belonged to the store manager, Mr. Fegato. He was sitting at a desk covered with brightly wrapped presents. While the twins watched, Mr. Fegato ripped one of the presents open. He glanced inside the box and then tossed it onto the floor. It landed on top of a pile of half-opened presents.

The twins' eyes grew wide.

Jessica forgot all about the lost purse. "Don't you like your presents?" she asked.

"They're not for *me*," the store manager complained. "They're for the *store*. They're sent by people who want to do business with Evelyn's. Not one of these presents is from someone who loves me."

"Oh," Jessica said. Mr. Fegato gave her the creeps. "Let's get out of here," she whispered to Elizabeth.

"Not yet," Elizabeth whispered back. "Is this the Lost and Found?" she asked politely. "We lost a purse. It has all of our money in it."

33

"I'll keep an eye out for it," Mr. Fegato said. Jessica thought he sounded as if he had said that a thousand times before. "Now get out of here."

Jessica and Elizabeth backed out of the office. They closed the door behind them.

"That man is not nice," Elizabeth said.

"He's the biggest meanie I've ever met," Jessica said.

"Let's go meet Mom and Dad," Elizabeth suggested.

"Mom and Dad!" Jessica said. "I forgot all about them. I guess we must be late by now."

"Very late," Elizabeth said.

The twins hurried to the seventh floor. They looked around for Mr. and Mrs. Wakefield. But their parents weren't there. Neither was Steven.

Elizabeth sank down onto a couch that was on display. "They're gone," she said. "We should have come up here a long time ago."

"I'm sorry," Jessica said. "I just didn't

35

want to come until we had a present for Mom."

"I know," Elizabeth said. "I didn't, either. It's not your fault."

Jessica sat down next to Elizabeth. "Mom always says to stay in one place if we get lost."

"I know," Elizabeth said. "I guess we have to wait here."

Jessica and Elizabeth waited. And waited. And waited.

"My stomach just growled," Jessica told Elizabeth after a long time. "It must be past dinnertime."

Elizabeth yawned. "I'm sleepy."

"Me, too," Jessica said.

"The store is emptying out," Elizabeth said.

"I hope Mom and Dad find us soon," Jessica said.

Elizabeth was staring at a fluffy feather bed that was on display. Jessica looked at it, too. It looked very comfy.

After what seemed like hours,

Elizabeth got up, walked over to the bed, and climbed in.

"Make room for me," Jessica told Elizabeth. She climbed into the bed and sank deep into the feathers.

Lying down, Jessica couldn't see the rest of the store. *I guess that means nobody can see us, either,* Jessica thought. Then she fell sound asleep.

When Jessica woke up, Elizabeth was shaking her.

"Get up!" Elizabeth cried. "Something terrible has happened!"

CHAPTER 5

911 Nonsense

"What's going on?" Jessica asked. "It's so dark!"

"I think the store is closed," Elizabeth replied.

"Closed?" Jessica repeated. "That's impossible." She climbed off the bed and looked around. "I don't see anyone," she reported. "Most of the lights are turned off. I think only the ones on the Christmas decorations are still on."

"Do you think we're locked inside?" Elizabeth asked. She was afraid.

"I guess we'd better go downstairs and see," Jessica said. Elizabeth crawled out of the feather bed. The twins joined hands. They started to walk down the aisle of the housewares department.

In the dark, the store looked different. There were spooky shadows everywhere. All the noisy shoppers were gone. The store seemed very still and quiet.

Elizabeth found herself tiptoeing. If she walked normally, her footsteps sounded awfully loud.

"Look at the escalator," Jessica whispered.

"It's stopped!" Elizabeth whispered back. "Now I *know* the store is closed!"

The twins peeked over the edge of the escalator.

"Do you think we can use it?" Elizabeth asked.

Jessica shrugged. "Why not? It's just like a staircase now."

Still holding hands, the twins took a cautious step onto the escalator. They stopped and waited. Nothing happened.

"It's fine," Elizabeth decided.

The twins hurried all the way down to

the first floor. The front entrance had a big gate pulled over it. The gate was held down by a huge padlock.

"We're definitely locked in," Elizabeth said.

"What should we do?" Jessica asked.

"I guess we ought to call for help," Elizabeth replied.

"Help!" Jessica screamed.

"No," Elizabeth said. "I meant on the telephone."

Jessica giggled. "I guess that makes sense."

The twins walked up to the third floor. They remembered passing a row of telephones there.

Elizabeth picked up one of the phones. Then she put it down. "We don't have any money."

"Oh, no," Jessica said. "I forgot. What do we do now?"

"We can still make an emergency phone call," Elizabeth said. "There's no charge for those."

Elizabeth picked up the phone and dialed 911.

"Emergency operator," came a businesslike voice. "Where are you, and what is the nature of your emergency?"

"Um . . ." Elizabeth said. "We're at Evelyn's—the new department store. Me and my sister are locked inside."

The operator didn't say anything for a few seconds. Then she started to laugh.

"I get it!" the operator said. "It's Christmas Eve and you're locked in a department store. Ha, ha, ha!"

"This is not a joke!" Elizabeth insisted.

"Right," the operator said. "And I'm Santa Claus. Listen, have a good time locked in there. Shop until you drop!" Then she hung up.

"What did she say?" asked Jessica.

"She told us to have a good time," Elizabeth replied.

Jessica groaned. "Is there anyone else we can call for free?"

Elizabeth squinted at the instructions

41

on the telephone. Luckily, she was a good reader.

"We can call home collect," Elizabeth said.

"What does that mean?" Jessica asked.

"I think it means that the person we call has to pay," Elizabeth explained.

"That's OK," Jessica said. "Mom and Dad won't mind if we call collect. This is an emergency."

Elizabeth looked at the directions on the phone again. Then she picked up the receiver. She dialed "0" and then her home phone number.

"Please say your name," a recorded voice demanded.

"Elizabeth."

There was a long pause.

Finally, the recorded voice came back. "We're sorry," it said. "But we have reached an answering machine. Please try your call again later."

"Nobody's home," Elizabeth told Jessica as she hung up the telephone.

"Maybe they haven't had time to get there yet," Jessica said. "I don't know how long we were asleep. But it's a pretty long drive home."

"I guess we're really stuck in here," Elizabeth said. "At least for a little while."

Jessica glanced around the dark, shadowy store. "I'm afraid," she whispered.

"Me, too," Elizabeth answered.

CHAPTER 6

Sugarplum Visions

"Maybe it's silly to be afraid," Jessica said bravely. "We're all alone in here. What could hurt us?"

"Nothing, I guess," Elizabeth agreed. "We're the only ones in the whole store."

Jessica's eyes lit up. "Did you hear what you just said?" she asked. "We have the entire store to ourselves! We can do whatever we want!"

"Except get out," Elizabeth said.

"Someone will find us soon," Jessica said. "Until then, we might as well have fun."

"What should we do?" Elizabeth asked.

"Eat!" Jessica said.

"But we don't have any money," Elizabeth pointed out.

"When Mom and Dad find us, they'll pay," Jessica said.

"That's dishonest," Elizabeth said. "We can't just take something and promise to pay for it later."

"Why not?" Jessica asked.

"It's like stealing!" Elizabeth said.

"Are you hungry or not?" Jessica asked.

"I'm starving," Elizabeth admitted.

"Then, come on," Jessica said. She marched off toward the elevators.

Elizabeth ran after Jessica.

"We can go to the snack bar," Jessica told Elizabeth. "Remember when we were shopping with Steven? We saw it on the eighth floor."

"Fine," Elizabeth said. She pushed the up button in front of the elevators.

The twins waited and waited.

"These elevators sure are slow," Jessica said.

"It's weird," Elizabeth said. "I thought the elevator would come right away. Nobody else is using them."

"I bet they're turned off!" Jessica said.

"You can turn elevators off?" Elizabeth asked.

"Sure," Jessica said. "Haven't you ever noticed the rows of locks elevators have inside? You can turn them off with a key."

"That means we need a key to turn them back on," Elizabeth said.

"I guess we have to walk," Jessica said.

The twins headed for the escalators. They climbed all the way up to the eighth floor.

"Whew," Elizabeth said when they got there. "That was a long walk."

"Now I'm really hungry," Jessica said.

"It looks really different up here," Elizabeth commented. The snack bar was all cleaned up. The chairs were turned upside down on top of the tables.

Elizabeth turned two chairs over.

Jessica walked behind the counter and opened one of the big freezer doors.

"Whoa!" Jessica exclaimed. "Check this out."

Elizabeth walked around the counter and peeked into the freezer. "Wow!" she said.

The twins stared at the wonderful things inside: hundreds of frozen pizzas, hamburger patties, and bags of french fries. There was an entire row of enormous containers of ice cream.

"Help me get this out," Jessica said. She started to struggle with a container of chocolate-chip ice cream.

Elizabeth started to tug on the container, too. Finally it fell out of the freezer and landed upright on the floor. The top of the container came all the way up to the twins' waists.

"Now all I need is a spoon," Jessica said.

Elizabeth laughed. "I think we should use bowls."

"Why?" Jessica asked.

Elizabeth peeked into the freezer. "So that we can put hot fudge, butterscotch, whipped cream, nuts, and a cherry on top of the ice cream."

"I'll find the bowls," Jessica said.

A few minutes later, the twins sat down with the hugest ice-cream sundaes imaginable. They did not say anything for several minutes. They were too busy eating.

"That was good," Elizabeth said when she finished.

"Definitely," Jessica agreed. "Do you know what we need now?"

"No, what?" Elizabeth said.

"Dessert!" Jessica said. She got up and poked around behind the counter. "I found some cookies! Yum, they're peanut butter."

Jessica handed a cookie to Elizabeth. She took a big bite of another one. "This is the best Christmas Eve dinner we've ever had," Jessica announced.

Elizabeth put her cookie down without tasting it.

"What's the matter?" Jessica asked.

"I'm not hungry anymore," Elizabeth said. She looked ready to cry.

"Why not?" Jessica asked.

"Because we're stuck in a department store *on Christmas Eve*," Elizabeth said. "Why did Mom and Dad leave us here?"

Jessica shook her head. "I don't know. But it stinks." She put her cookie down, too. "Now we won't be home to hear Dad read *The Night Before Christmas*."

"I bet Dad isn't reading *The Night Before Christmas*," Elizabeth said. "He's probably out somewhere looking for us. And he's probably really worried."

Jessica nodded. "Mom, too."

"And Steven," Elizabeth said.

Jessica smiled. "I bet Steven isn't worried about us."

"Sure he is," Elizabeth said. "If Mom and Dad don't find us in time, he won't get to open his presents tomorrow morning."

Jessica laughed. "You're right. Steven

is *really* worried about us." But then Jessica's smile faded. "Do you think Mom and Dad meant to leave us here?"

"No way," Elizabeth said.

"I guess not," Jessica agreed. "After all, we were the ones who were so late."

"Come on," Elizabeth said. "Let's clean up this mess."

Jessica put away the syrup, whipped cream, and nuts. Elizabeth dragged a chair over to the sink and washed the dirty dishes. Then the twins worked together to lift the enormous container of ice cream into the freezer. They put their chairs back on top of the tables.

"All finished," Elizabeth announced.

At that second, all of the lights on the Christmas decorations suddenly went out. Everything was pitch-black!

CHAPTER 7

Holiday Finery

"Why did all the lights go out?" Elizabeth asked.

"I don't know." Jessica sounded frightened. "But it's really dark in here."

Elizabeth reached out and took Jessica's hand.

Jessica started to laugh.

"What's so funny?" said Elizabeth.

"I know what happened," Jessica explained. "At Lila's house, the lights are on a timer. They turn themselves on and off." Lila Fowler was one of Jessica's best friends. She lived in a big mansion.

"The store must have the same thing," Elizabeth said.

"Right," Jessica agreed. "We don't have anything to worry about."

"I can see a little better now," Elizabeth reported. "I think my eyes are adjusting to the dark. And a few tiny lights are still on. Like that one in the EXIT sign."

"I think those are emergency lights," Jessica said. "They never go out."

"Are you afraid?" Elizabeth asked. Jessica was usually terrified of the dark.

"No," Jessica said. "I just had a terrific idea. We can play dress-up. With ball gowns! And I think I saw some wedding dresses on the fourth floor."

"Jessica—" Elizabeth started.

"And shoes!" Jessica said. She was already heading for the escalator. "The shoe department has hundreds of pairs of grown-up shoes. And we can give each other makeovers at the makeup counters!"

Elizabeth hurried after her sister. "No, we can't," she insisted. "We can't play with dresses and shoes and

53

makeup that don't belong to us."

"It's not like we're going to take the stuff," Jessica said. "We're just going to borrow it."

"But—" Elizabeth tried again.

"Women come to stores all the time to try things on," Jessica said. "That's all we're going to do."

"Oh. OK," Elizabeth agreed.

"Great," Jessica said. "Formal dresses are on four."

"How do you know that?" Elizabeth asked. "We haven't even been on the fourth floor yet."

Jessica shrugged. "I just know."

The twins found the formal-dress department exactly where Jessica said it would be.

"You're amazing," Elizabeth told Jessica.

"Try this on," Jessica said. She took a green dress off the rack. Sequins were sewn all over it.

Elizabeth pulled on the dress over her jeans and T-shirt.

"You look like a mermaid," Jessica told her.

Elizabeth giggled. "Now I get to pick out a dress for you." She examined the racks and pulled out a pink dress with a huge poofy skirt.

"It looks like something a princess would wear," Jessica said. She slipped the dress over her head. Elizabeth helped her zip it up.

Jessica spun around in a circle. "I'm going to get a dress just like this one when I grow up. Come on! Let's go try out the makeup now."

"OK," Elizabeth agreed. She didn't feel like arguing anymore. She was having too much fun.

On one of the makeup counters, Jessica found a mirror with a light on it. "Now we'll be able to see what we're doing," she announced as she turned it on.

"Look at this lipstick," Elizabeth exclaimed. "It's purple!"

"Cool," Jessica said. "You should try it."

"No way!" Elizabeth put the purple lipstick back. She chose one that was pale pink.

Jessica smeared on a cherry-red lipstick.

Elizabeth watched while her sister experimented with eye shadow, mascara, eyeliner, eyebrow pencil, blush, and powder.

"Do I look pretty?" Jessica asked, batting her eyelashes.

"No!" Elizabeth said. "You look like a clown."

"Thanks a lot," Jessica said.

"It's true," Elizabeth insisted.

"Maybe if I just rub some of this in," Jessica said.

Elizabeth shook her head. "I think you'd better wash it off. Come on. Let's find the bathroom."

"OK," Jessica said. "My face is starting to itch anyway."

The twins found the bathroom on the third floor. Jessica scrubbed the makeup off her face. On their way out of the bathroom, the girls passed the manager's office.

Through the door, Jessica could see the messy pile of presents. It covered the store manager's desk and spilled over onto the floor.

"I can't believe Mr. Fegato threw his presents around like that," Elizabeth said.

"Let's pick them up," Jessica suggested.

The office door was unlocked. The twins let themselves in. They picked all the presents up off the floor and put them in a neat pile.

Elizabeth found a tiny box near the garbage can. It had a big letter attached to it. The store manager had not even unwrapped the box, even though it said "To Mr. Fegato" right on the top.

"I wonder what's in here," Elizabeth said.

"Don't open it," Jessica warned. "It's probably itching powder. That's what I'd like to get Mr. Fegato for Christmas."

"This letter might help us," Elizabeth said.

"How?" Jessica asked.

"Well, this present is for Mr. Fegato," Elizabeth explained. "Maybe the letter will tell us where he lives."

"So?" Jessica asked.

"If we knew where he lived, we could call him," Elizabeth went on.

"Oh, I get it," Jessica said. "Crank calls."

"That's not what I meant," Elizabeth said.

"What, then?" Jessica asked.

"We could get him to come let us out," Elizabeth said.

"Right!" Jessica said. "That's an excellent idea."

Elizabeth opened the letter. She read for a second and then let out a gasp.

"What is it?" Jessica asked.

"The letter is from Mr. Fegato's daughter," Elizabeth explained.

59

"What does it say?" Jessica asked.

"Dear Daddy," Elizabeth read. "Things are fine here in New Jersey."

"New Jersey?" Jessica repeated. "That's really far away!"

Elizabeth nodded. Then she continued to read. "Mommy is fine. I miss you. I wish I could see you. You love Christmas more than anyone else. Love, Maggie."

"Mr. Fegato loves Christmas?" Jessica asked.

"I guess he used to . . ." Elizabeth said thoughtfully.

"Maybe now that his daughter is so far away, he's unhappy," Jessica suggested.

"He's all alone," Elizabeth added.

"I feel sorry for—"

Jessica stopped what she was saying. "What's that?" she whispered.

Loud music had suddenly started to play.

Before Elizabeth could answer, the music stopped.

"I think it was coming from a couple floors away," Jessica said.

"There's a stereo department upstairs," Elizabeth said. "Remember?"

Jessica shivered. "The store wouldn't put *music* on a timer, would they?" she asked.

"No," Elizabeth admitted.

Just then the twins heard several loud crashes.

"Jessica," Elizabeth said in a shaky voice. "I think—I think Evelyn's has a ghost."

CHAPTER 8

A Messy Intruder

The twins held their breath and waited.

"I don't hear anything," Jessica whispered.

"Me neither," Elizabeth said.

"It's getting creepy in here," Jessica complained. "I wish someone would come and find us."

"It must be getting pretty late," Elizabeth said. "Someone will find us when they open the store in the morning."

Jessica suddenly looked even more miserable. "But tomorrow's Christmas. The store will be closed."

"That means nobody will find us until

the day after tomorrow," Elizabeth said.

"I want to go home," Jessica said.

"Me, too," Elizabeth agreed. "But we can't do anything about it. We might as well go down to the toy department and play."

"OK," Jessica agreed. "What are you going to do with Mr. Fegato's gift?"

"I'll leave it right here on his desk," Elizabeth decided. "That way, he'll find it when he comes back to work."

"But by then Christmas will be over," Jessica commented.

"It's the best we can do," Elizabeth said. She put the box down on Mr. Fegato's desk. The twins headed toward the first floor.

"Look," Jessica said as they passed a display case.

Elizabeth peeked inside. "Mom's jewelry box."

"I wish we could get it," Jessica said.

"Mom would love to unwrap that on Christmas morning," Elizabeth agreed.

"Well, she couldn't do that even if we could afford the jewelry box," Jessica

63

said. "We're not going to be home for Christmas morning."

"No," Elizabeth said. "But at least we have each other. I would hate to be all alone on Christmas like Mr. Fegato."

Jessica let out a deep sigh. "Come on. Let's go to the toy department."

As soon as Jessica walked by the giant nutcrackers and into the toy department, she started to feel happier. "Let's play video games," she suggested. "There's no line now."

"Great idea," Elizabeth agreed.

Evelyn's had a dozen video games on display. The twins worked their way down the row, trying every one.

"I can't wait to tell Steven about this," Elizabeth said.

Jessica grinned. "He's going to be super jealous."

"Now what?" Elizabeth asked when they had tried all of the video games.

"You decide," Jessica suggested.

Elizabeth surveyed the toy department.

She walked toward the beautiful, gleaming cars. "I bet I could beat you in a car race," Elizabeth challenged Jessica.

Jessica laughed. "You don't even know how to drive."

"Which car do you want?" Elizabeth asked.

"The red one," Jessica said immediately.

"I'll take the blue one with white stripes," Elizabeth decided. She reached into the cars and removed the ribbons across their seats. The twins climbed in.

Elizabeth found a key in the car's ignition. She turned it. "Zoom!" went the blue convertible.

"All right!" Jessica yelled. "Let's race to the elevators and back."

"On the count of three," Elizabeth called out.

"One, two, three," the twins yelled together—and they were off!

Jessica and Elizabeth raced by a massive stuffed polar bear, past the playhouse in the center of the toy department, under

the slide of the jungle gym, by a tall stack of books, through a Lego castle, and out of the toy department.

Jessica was in the lead.

The twins sped down a long corridor, under the glow of the EXIT sign, and past the stopped elevators.

Jessica made a slow, careful turn. But Elizabeth skidded into hers without touching the brakes.

The drivers headed back to the toy department with Elizabeth in the lead.

The twins raced past the giant nutcrackers. Seconds later, they zoomed up to the place where the race had begun.

"I win!" Jessica and Elizabeth yelled at the same time.

"That was fun," Jessica said as she climbed out of her car.

"It was," Elizabeth said. "But now I'm hungry again."

"Let's get a snack," Jessica suggested.

"Beat you," Elizabeth yelled. She ran toward the escalators.

67

"No fair," Jessica called as she started to run after her sister. "You had a head start!"

The twins raced all the way back up to the eighth floor.

"I win," Elizabeth said, panting, when they finally reached the snack bar.

"What's that?" Jessica asked. She pointed to one of the counters. It was a complete mess.

"It looks like Steven has been eating here," Elizabeth said.

"Who would have messed up the snack bar like this?" Jessica asked.

"The night guard?" Elizabeth suggested.

"I don't think there is one tonight," Jessica said. "We haven't seen one yet. And it is Christmas Eve. The guard is probably home with her family."

"Well, we didn't do it," Elizabeth said.

"Ghosts don't eat," Jessica pointed out. "At least, I don't think they do. . . ."

"So who else is in the store?" Elizabeth wondered.

CHAPTER 9

A Bumbling Thief

"Jessica," Elizabeth said. "I don't think the person who was up here works at Evelyn's. That means he shouldn't be in the store."

"Maybe it's someone who got stuck, like us," Jessica suggested.

"Could be," Elizabeth agreed. "But just in case, I think we should find him before he finds us."

"OK," Jessica said. She looked around the snack bar. "Hey, Elizabeth. I think I found a clue."

Jessica walked toward the escalator, bent down, and picked something up.

"What is it?" Elizabeth asked.

"The wrapper off a candy cane," Jessica said. "Someone threw it on the floor."

"Someone sloppy," Elizabeth said.

"Like the person who made the mess on the counter," Jessica said.

Elizabeth grinned. "Right! And look— I think I see something on the floor at the bottom of the escalator. Maybe it's another wrapper."

The twins walked down to the seventh floor. The shiny object Elizabeth had spotted *was* another candy wrapper. A little farther down the aisle, the twins noticed a couple of display chairs knocked over.

A piece of just-chewed gum was stuck to the handrail of the escalator leading to the sixth floor. Once they got to six, Jessica and Elizabeth could hear someone in the stereo department.

Elizabeth put her fingers to her lips.

Jessica nodded.

Quietly, the twins tiptoed toward the stereo department. They peeked in—and saw a man inside!

The man was dressed in black, except for a bright-pink baseball cap. He was mumbling to himself.

The man pushed a cart toward the display of stereos. He pulled a CD player off the shelf and unplugged it. He tried to put the CD player into the cart, but he missed. It fell on his foot instead.

"Drat!" the man exclaimed.

"It's a thief," Jessica whispered.

Elizabeth nodded. "He's kind of clumsy."

While the twins watched, the thief backed up into a switch. Music blared. Cursing again, the thief spun around and switched the music off.

"He's been making the noises we heard," Jessica whispered.

"We've got to hide," Elizabeth whispered back. "He could be dangerous."

Jessica nodded. "Let's go."

The girls got up, tiptoed a few paces, and started to run.

Jessica's foot slipped out from under

71

her. She hit the ground hard. "Aggh!" Jessica groaned.

Elizabeth turned around. "Are you OK?" she whispered. As she helped Jessica up, Elizabeth glanced back toward the stereo department. The thief had come out. He was rushing toward her.

"Run!" Jessica yelled.

CHAPTER 10

Toy-Department Chase

"Hurry up, Jessica," Elizabeth called.

"I'm coming," Jessica answered. She ran after her sister as fast as she could.

"You won't get away!" the thief yelled.

Jessica shivered at the sound of the thief's voice. He sounded scary.

Elizabeth sprinted down the escalator.

Jessica was right behind her.

The thief was right behind her.

But by the time the twins got down to one, they had left the thief a few floors behind. He really couldn't run that fast.

"Where should we go?" Elizabeth said, breathing hard.

"Into the toy department," Jessica said. "There's lots of places to hide in there."

The twins ran into the toy department and looked around.

"Come on," Jessica said. She ran over to the jungle gym and crawled into a big yellow plastic tunnel.

"Make room for me," Elizabeth said. She crawled in after her sister.

A second later, the twins heard the thief stomp into the toy department.

Jessica closed her eyes, held her breath, and hoped the thief wouldn't find them.

Elizabeth gasped.

Jessica opened her eyes.

The thief was peering into the end of the plastic tunnel. He looked hard at the twins and started to laugh. Then he disappeared.

"What's he doing?" Elizabeth asked.

Jessica shook her head. "I don't know."

The thief came back. He was holding a butterfly net. The thief poked the net down the tunnel.

"Ouch," Elizabeth exclaimed. The thief had poked her in the ribs with the net.

Elizabeth moved closer to Jessica.

Jessica moved back to give Elizabeth more room.

The thief poked Elizabeth again. The girls moved back a little more. The thief poked again. The girls moved again. Slowly, the twins got farther and farther away from the thief and the butterfly net.

Jessica was watching the thief. Without paying attention to what she was doing, she moved back one more time. But Jessica had run out of room! She popped out of the tunnel and landed on the floor of the toy department.

The thief swooped down and grabbed her. "Got you," he growled.

Jessica struggled with the thief. But she couldn't get out of his grasp.

"Now you come out!" the thief told Elizabeth. Holding Jessica under one arm, he bent down to peek into the tunnel.

Elizabeth scooted down the tunnel as fast as she could. She crawled out of the other side and sprinted across the room.

A playhouse stood in the center of the toy department. It looked just like a real house, but it was tiny and made out of cardboard.

Elizabeth ran inside.

The thief dragged Jessica over to the playhouse. He peeked through the door. But he was too big to get in.

Elizabeth pressed herself against the wall that was farthest away from the door.

"Hmm," the thief said. Then, with a sudden movement, he pushed Jessica in with Elizabeth and slammed the cardboard door.

The twins exchanged surprised looks.

"Are you OK?" Elizabeth asked.

"Yes," Jessica said. "But I don't understand why he let me go. This is the perfect hiding place."

Elizabeth shrugged. "It doesn't make sense."

Then the twins felt the thief push something heavy up against the playhouse.

"Oh, no," Elizabeth said. "He's blocking the door."

"We're stuck," Jessica groaned.

"Now you two will be out of my way," the thief said.

Jessica peeked out of the playhouse's tiny window. Only one of her eyes fit into the opening, but Jessica could see the thief. He was pushing a big box up against the door, but that wasn't what upset Jessica the most. Her pink purse was hanging around his neck!

"You're the man who pushed me," Jessica yelled. "You stole my purse!"

The thief laughed. "That's right," he sneered. "By the way, I really like your purse. It makes a nice necklace."

"Let me look," Elizabeth said.

Jessica moved to one side, and Elizabeth peeked through the window. "That money is for our mother's Christmas present," she yelled.

"Boo-hoo," the thief said.

"He's leaving," Elizabeth reported.

"What a meanie," Jessica fumed. "We have to stop him. He's going to steal everything in the whole store. Just like he stole my purse!"

"But we're stuck in here," Elizabeth said.

"Then let's get out!" Jessica insisted.

The twins looked around. They tried pushing on the door, but it was firmly blocked.

"The windows are much too small to crawl through," Jessica commented.

"What about this fireplace?" Elizabeth said. She got down on her hands and knees and peeked up the cardboard chimney. "There's a hole here!" she exclaimed. "It goes all the way to the roof.

80

And I think it's big enough to crawl through."

Jessica got down next to Elizabeth. "All right!"

"I'll give you a boost," Elizabeth suggested.

Jessica got up on Elizabeth's shoulders. She wiggled into the chimney up to her knees.

Elizabeth struggled to her feet.

Jessica squeezed up the cardboard chimney.

"Are you OK?" Elizabeth asked.

"I can almost reach," Jessica replied.

Stretching as far as she could, Jessica got her fingers around the outside of the chimney. Elizabeth pushed on her feet.

Finally Jessica pulled herself out onto the playhouse's roof. "I'm out," she yelled down the chimney. "I'll unblock the door!"

Jessica peeked off the roof. It was a long way to the floor. She climbed down carefully, using the boxes the thief had pushed in front of the door as a ladder.

Once she was on the ground, Jessica moved the boxes away from the door one by one.

"Thank you!" Elizabeth said when she was free.

"No problem," Jessica told her.

"The thief will probably be back any minute," Elizabeth said.

Jessica nodded. "We have to be ready to catch him when he comes. But how can we do that?"

"We have to set a trap," Elizabeth replied.

"With what?" Jessica asked.

"Whatever we can find," Elizabeth said. "Look around."

Jessica turned in a circle. "I see toys."

"Then that's what we'll use," Elizabeth said.

CHAPTER 11

A Sticky Trap

"There," Elizabeth said. "It's perfect."

"Our trap is finished," Jessica said. "Now all we need is the thief."

"Where do you think he is?" Elizabeth asked.

Jessica shrugged. "I don't know. But all we have to do now is wait for him to come back."

"I don't think that's a good idea," Elizabeth said. "What if he just leaves?"

"You're right," Jessica agreed. "I don't want the thief to get away. Let's go find him."

Elizabeth took two walkie-talkies off a

shelf. She handed one to Jessica. "Put this on your belt. Then do what I do."

"No problem," Jessica said.

"One more thing," Elizabeth added. "Try not to fall this time."

"I'll try," Jessica agreed.

"Then let's go," Elizabeth said.

The twins tiptoed out of the toy department. They crept up to the second floor and looked around for the thief. They found him in the jewelry department. He was loading glittering necklaces into a big box.

Without getting too close to the thief, Elizabeth pushed a button on her walkie-talkie. It let out a squawk.

The thief's head shot up. "Who's there?" he whispered, tiptoeing toward the sound.

The twins didn't answer. Instead, they ran toward the escalator. Then Jessica made the noise with her walkie-talkie.

The thief followed it.

The twins dashed down the escalator

as fast as they could. They hid behind the enormous Christmas tree on the first floor. Then Elizabeth made another noise with her walkie-talkie.

The thief followed.

Slowly, the twins led him all the way back to the entrance of the toy department. They stood behind the nutcrackers and held their breath.

Cautiously, the thief stepped inside the toy department.

"Aggh!" he yelled as he slipped. The twins had spread marbles all over the floor. The thief landed bottom first in a vat of gooey green slime.

Jessica ran into the toy department. She climbed to the top of the slide. Using a massive water gun, she squirted chocolate syrup into the thief's face.

"Cut it out!" the thief yelled. "I can't see anything!"

While the thief was trying to rub the chocolate out of his eyes, Elizabeth ran over to him. She tied up the thief with

licorice rope. It was the only rope the twins could find.

Jessica turned on a tape recorder. It started to blare Brenda songs.

The thief covered his ears. "Have mercy," he begged. "I can't stand that stupid pink rhino. Turn it off!"

"In your dreams!" Jessica yelled.

The twins exchanged a high five.

CHAPTER 12

Jessica Sounds the Alarm

"Now what?" Jessica asked.

"I'll guard the thief," Elizabeth suggested. "You go call the police."

"All right," Jessica agreed. She ran toward the entrance of the toy department.

"Wait," Elizabeth called after her. "Get your purse first. You can try Mom and Dad again."

"Good idea," Jessica said with a grin. She ran up to the thief and plucked her purse off his neck.

"Yuck," Elizabeth said.

Jessica smiled. "It *is* a little sticky," she reported. "But the money inside is fine."

"Great," Elizabeth said. "Now, hurry up. I want to get out of here."

"OK," Jessica agreed. She ran out of the toy department and up to the third floor. Jessica picked up a telephone and dialed 911.

"Emergency operator," came a businesslike voice. "Where are you, and what is the nature of your emergency?"

"I caught a thief!" Jessica announced proudly.

"How old are you, honey?" the operator asked.

"Seven," Jessica replied.

"What's your name?" the operator asked.

"Jessica."

"Well now, Jessica," the operator said, "I think it's wonderful that you caught a thief. But isn't it time for you to be asleep? It must be past your bedtime."

"I guess it is," Jessica admitted. "But I've been busy catching the thief I told you about. Can you send over the police? I don't want him to get away."

"Jessica," the operator said. "You are being extremely naughty. This phone line is only for emergencies. While you're playing cops and robbers, someone out there might really need my help. Good night, now. And happy holidays."

"I'm telling you—" Jessica started. But it was too late. The operator had already hung up.

Jessica sighed. She pulled some change out of her purse and put it in the phone. She dialed the Wakefields' number.

The phone rang five times. Then the answering machine picked up. Jessica hung up without leaving a message.

"Where could Mom and Dad be now?" Jessica muttered. She headed toward the toy department, feeling very sad.

Back on the first floor, Jessica spotted a fire alarm. *Should I pull it?* she wondered. On one hand, it was the wrong thing to do: Evelyn's wasn't on fire. But there *was* a real emergency. And Jessica had tried to call the operator. The fire alarm might be the only way the twins were going to get help. Not to mention get home in time for Christmas.

Jessica took a deep breath. She pulled the alarm.

Elizabeth was watching the thief.

The thief was watching Elizabeth.

The fire alarm went off.

Elizabeth jumped.

The sprinklers came on.

"What is that?" Elizabeth exclaimed with surprise.

The thief looked up—and smiled. He turned his face toward the ceiling. The sprinkler started to wash the chocolate syrup out of his eyes.

Elizabeth could see that the water was also making the licorice soft.

The thief plugged his ears. "I can't hear Brenda now!" he yelled at Elizabeth. He started to wiggle loose.

Elizabeth felt panicky. The thief was going to get free. The thief was going to get *her*. Where was Jessica? Where were the police?

Elizabeth walked a few steps toward the entrance of the toy department. She peered down the hallway, searching for Jessica.

Jessica came running toward Elizabeth. "Watch out!" she screamed.

Elizabeth turned back toward the thief.

It was too late.

The thief jumped up and grabbed Elizabeth from behind.

Elizabeth screamed.

"Let her go!" Jessica yelled.

"Back off," the thief ordered Jessica. "If you don't, I'll send your sister to the North Pole."

CHAPTER 13

Santa to the Rescue

Jessica moved back toward the entrance of the toy department. She ducked down behind a shelf, pulled several packages off a nearby rack, and ripped them open.

Something has to distract the thief for a few seconds, Jessica thought. *Then I'll get him.*

The thief was holding on to Elizabeth with one hand. With the other hand, he was pushing his cart full of stolen stuff. He was slowly moving toward an emergency exit. The thief was about to escape, and he was going to take Elizabeth with him!

Jessica couldn't do anything to stop him.

But suddenly she heard a sound coming from the back of the toy department.

It sounded like sleigh bells! And a jolly "Ho, ho, ho!"

The thief heard the sound, too. He turned to look.

Jessica saw her opening. She quickly loaded the slingshot she had just unwrapped, took aim—and beaned the thief with a Brenda action figure.

The thief slumped to the ground.

Elizabeth slipped out of his grasp and ran across the toy department.

The twins shared a hug.

At that instant, the lights came on.

"What's going on here?" an angry voice demanded.

It was the police! A bunch of firemen were right behind them. Mr. Fegato, the store manager, was right behind them. And the Wakefields were right behind *him*.

"That man is a thief!" Jessica yelled, pointing.

The police hurried over to handcuff the thief.

"Boy," a policewoman with brown hair said. "This guy sure has sticky fingers."

"Yeah," a policeman replied. "It looks as if he's been playing in a candy factory."

The thief was starting to wake up. "I've been pulling jobs for years," he muttered. "I've never seen anything like these girls. They're a menace."

The policewoman helped the thief stand up. "Tell it to the judge," she said, leading him toward the door.

One of the policemen started to dust for fingerprints. Another was snapping photographs.

Mr. Wakefield, Mrs. Wakefield, and Steven rushed up to the twins.

"Are you OK?" Mrs. Wakefield asked.

"What's going on here?" Mr. Wakefield said at the same time.

"We caught a thief," Jessica said proudly.

"We're fine," Elizabeth added.

"You shrimps caught a thief?" Steven asked. "What a joke."

"We did!" Elizabeth insisted.

"That's pretty funny," Steven said.

Just then another policeman came hurrying in. "I found the thief's van," he reported. "It's stuffed full of jewelry, stereos, all kinds of expensive stuff. The Evelyn's tags are still on everything."

"See?" Jessica said to Steven. "I told you so!"

"Have you been in the store all this time?" Mrs. Wakefield asked.

"Yes," Elizabeth replied. "The thief stole Jessica's purse. We were looking for it, so we got to housewares late. We were waiting and waiting for you. Finally we fell asleep on one of the display beds. When we woke up, the store was closed."

"That explains why we couldn't find you," Mr. Wakefield said.

Steven cleared his throat. "Um—I'm sorry I left you guys alone," he told the

97

twins. "I guess it was kind of my fault that you got lost."

Jessica and Elizabeth exchanged looks.

"That's OK," Jessica said.

"We forgive you," Elizabeth added. "Being locked in the store was kind of fun. At least, part of the time."

"Where did *you* go?" Jessica asked her family. "We called home twice. Nobody was there."

"A few minutes after the store closed, the manager insisted that we leave," Mr. Wakefield said.

"He threw us out," Steven said.

"The manager told us that you couldn't still be inside," Mrs. Wakefield added. "We had already searched the entire store for you twice."

"After the manager made us leave, we went to the L.A. Police Department," Mr. Wakefield said. "We've been there ever since. A few minutes ago, one of the policemen told us a fire alarm had been pulled at Evelyn's. We had a feeling it was you."

"We called home several times," Mrs. Wakefield added. "But there were no messages on the answering machine."

"We didn't leave any messages," Jessica explained.

"We were really worried," Mr. Wakefield said.

"I'm sorry we caused so much trouble," Elizabeth said.

"I'm just glad everything is all right now," Mrs. Wakefield said.

"All right?" came the store manager's outraged voice. "The toy department is ruined!"

CHAPTER 14

The Jewelry Box

Elizabeth looked around. She had to admit that Mr. Fegato was right. The toy department did look pretty bad. There were marbles, chocolate syrup, licorice, and slime all over the floor. Plus, everything was soggy from the sprinkler.

"It's going to take days to clean this up!" Mr. Fegato's face was turning bright red. "I ought to have you two girls arrested!"

"Jessica," Elizabeth said, "I think we'd better tell him what we found."

"Found? Found?" the store manager bellowed. "What are you talking about now?"

"Tell him," Jessica said. "Fast!"

"Mr. Fegato," Elizabeth said in a polite voice, "may we talk to you, please?"

"Go ahead!" Mr. Fegato bellowed. "Talk!"

"Um—" Elizabeth said. "We want to talk to you *alone*."

"We need to show you something extremely important," Jessica added. "It's in your office."

Mr. Fegato looked furious. But he agreed to go upstairs with Elizabeth and Jessica.

Elizabeth turned to her family. "Would you mind waiting for us here? This is kind of personal."

"Don't worry about us," Mrs. Wakefield said. "Just don't get lost!"

"Promise," Elizabeth said, grinning.

Mr. Fegato turned on the elevator. He and the twins rode up to the third floor. "This had better be good," he muttered as he followed the twins into his office.

"It is," Jessica said. "Very good."

"We found this," Elizabeth explained. She handed Mr. Fegato the package from his daughter. "It was on the floor under the pile of presents."

"I don't have time to open gifts now," Mr. Fegato fumed. "Thanks to you kids, I have an entire toy department to clean up."

"Then just read the letter," Elizabeth suggested.

Impatiently, the store manager took the letter and started to read. Slowly, a huge smile spread over his face. He studied the letter for much longer than it took to read it.

"I'm very happy," Mr. Fegato finally told the twins. "This is the only gift I really wanted to get this holiday. I don't know how to repay you."

"You don't have to pay us," Elizabeth told him.

"But I insist!" Mr. Fegato said. "Why don't you pick out a reward for yourselves? Anything in the entire store!"

Elizabeth shook her head. "We really

don't want—*ouch!* Jessica! Why did you kick me?"

Jessica didn't answer Elizabeth's question. "There is one thing we would like," she told Mr. Fegato.

Elizabeth gave her sister a puzzled look.

"It's a wooden jewelry box," Jessica said. "With a blue satin lining."

"Right!" Elizabeth exclaimed. "It's not for us. We want to give it to our mother as a Christmas present."

"Let's go get it," Mr. Fegato suggested.

The twins led the store manager down to the second floor. They pointed out the jewelry box.

Mr. Fegato took it out of the display case. "Why don't I gift wrap this for you?" he suggested. "That way your mother won't see what it is."

"That sounds great," Elizabeth agreed.

A few minutes later, Mr. Fegato placed a box in Jessica's hands. It was covered with brilliant green paper, and it had an enormous red bow on it.

"It's beautiful," Jessica said.

"Can I do anything else for you?" Mr. Fegato asked.

"Yes," Jessica said. "We want to pay you for two sundaes from the snack bar. We got really hungry, so we helped ourselves."

"Forget it," Mr. Fegato said.

Jessica looked worried. "They were really *big* sundaes. And we also had a couple of cookies."

"Forget it," Mr. Fegato insisted. "Without you two, that thief would have stolen a lot of valuable things. The least I can do is pay for your ice cream!"

Elizabeth yawned. "I can't wait to get home."

"Me neither," Mr. Fegato said. "After all, it's almost Christmas."

"You mean, we didn't miss it?" Jessica asked.

Mr. Fegato shook his head. "It won't be midnight for more than an hour."

"I'm so happy," Elizabeth whispered

to Jessica in the elevator. "We're going to get home in time to hear Dad read *The Night Before Christmas*."

"It's going to be great," Jessica whispered back. "But we can't go yet. There's one more thing I want to do before we leave Evelyn's."

"What?" Elizabeth asked.

"I'll show you when we get downstairs," Jessica said.

When the twins got back to the toy department, Mrs. Wakefield was yawning.

"Are you kids ready to go?" Mr. Wakefield asked.

"Almost," Jessica replied. "We just need to find something. It will only take a few minutes."

"OK," Mrs. Wakefield agreed. She looked as if she was too tired to argue.

Elizabeth followed Jessica toward the back of the toy department. So did Steven.

"I can't believe you two caught a thief all by yourselves," Steven said. He sounded extremely jealous.

"Actually, we had a little help," Elizabeth said.

"Who helped you?" Steven asked.

"Santa Claus," Elizabeth told him.

Steven rolled his eyes. "Fine. Don't tell me."

"Hurry up!" Jessica yelled from farther down the aisle.

Steven stopped to examine a hockey stick.

Elizabeth ran to catch up with Jessica. "What are we looking for?" she asked.

"I want to find out what made the noise that distracted the thief," Jessica explained.

"Look," Elizabeth said. "There's a stuffed Santa in the middle of the last aisle."

Jessica hurried over and picked up the Santa. "He has a bell around his neck," she reported. Jessica shook the bell. It sounded just like the sleigh bell that had helped save Elizabeth.

Elizabeth reached out and rubbed the toy's fat belly.

"Ho, ho, ho," Santa said.

"This must have been it," Jessica decided. She sounded disappointed. "I was hoping it was the *real* Santa."

"Maybe it was," Elizabeth said. "After all, nobody was here to rub the toy's belly when we needed a distraction."

"Maybe Santa fell off the shelf," Jessica suggested. "He could have hit the floor belly first. That would have made him say 'Ho, ho, ho.' And it might have made his bell jiggle, too."

Elizabeth didn't look convinced. "Can you explain why Santa fell off the shelf at just the right second?"

Jessica looked puzzled for a second. Then she smiled. "That's easy to explain," she said. "It was Christmas magic!"